Toopy and Binoo™

Books inspired by the televised series

Library and Archives Canada
Cataloguing in Publication

Jolin, Dominique, 1964-
[Il était une fin. English]
Toopy's Story
(Toopy and Binoo)
Translation of: Il était une fin.
For children.

ISBN 978-1-55389-015-7

I. Tremblay, Carole, 1959- . II. Simon, Karen.
III. Title. IV. Title: Il était une fin. English.
V. Series: Jolin, Dominique, 1964- . Toopy and Binoo.
PS8569.O399I4213 2006   jC843'.54   C2006-940835-1
PS9569.O399I4213 2006

This text is adapted from an episode of the televised series *Toopy and
Binoo* produced by Spectra Animation Inc., with the participation of Treehouse.
Original script by Anne-Marie Perrotta and Tean Schultz
Writing director: Katherine Sandford

2006 © Spectra Animation Inc. All rights reserved.
From the collection Toopy and Binoo by Dominique Jolin published by
Dominique et compagnie, a division of Les éditions Héritage inc.
Toopy and Binoo is a trademark of Dominique et compagnie, a division
of Les éditions Héritage inc.

Collection director: Lucie Papineau
Artistic and graphic direction and *Toopy and Binoo*
typeface design by Primeau & Barey

Legal Deposit: 1st Quarter 2007
Bibliothèque et Archives nationales du Québec
National Library of Canada

Dominique et compagnie
300 Arran Street, Saint-Lambert, Quebec, Canada J4R 1K5
Tel: 514 875-0327 Fax: 450 672-5448
E-mail: dominiqueetcie@editionsheritage.com

www.dominiqueetcompagnie.com

Printed in China
10 9 8 7 6 5 4 3 2 1

We acknowledge the support of the Canada Council for the Arts for our publishing program.

We acknowledge the financial support of the Government of Canada through the
Book Publishing Industry Development Program (BPIDP) for our publishing activities.

Government of Québec – Publishing Program and Tax Credit Program – Gestion SODEC.

Toopy's Story

Text by Dominique Jolin and Carole Tremblay
English Text by Karen Simon

From the original script by Anne-Marie Perrotta and Tean Schultz
Illustrations taken from the televised series *Toopy and Binoo*

Click!

"Good night Binoo," says Toopy.

Click!

Binoo turns the light back on and shows a picture book to Toopy. "Oh, I get it. You want a story, right?" Toopy asks. "Well, okay, but just one. I'm reallllly tired!!!"

Toopy begins to read,
"Once upon a time…"
He yawns.
"There were two brave knights, Sir Toopy and Sir Binoo…"
He yawns again.
"That searched all over the kingdom for a dragon.
Suddenly, the two knights found one and bravely followed
it into the Enchanted Forest. Uh-oh, sorry Binoo, but
I can't finish the story… the last page is missing."

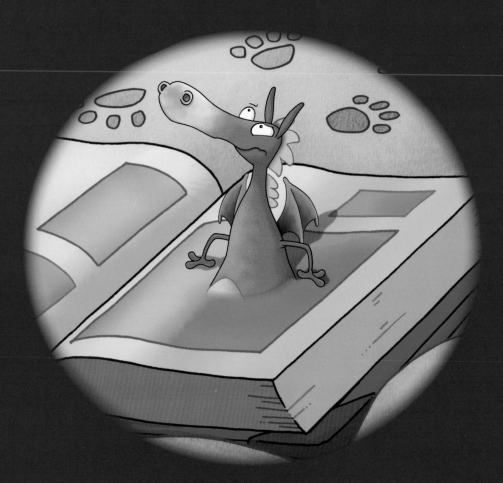

"But don't worry. I'll make up an ending."
Toopy yawns, then mumbles, "So the two brave
knights went home and went to bed.
The End."

Binoo doesn't like that ending.
And neither does the dragon.

So Toopy suggests,
"The two knights continued to follow the dragon. They had walked for two hours in the Enchanted Forest when all of a sudden...

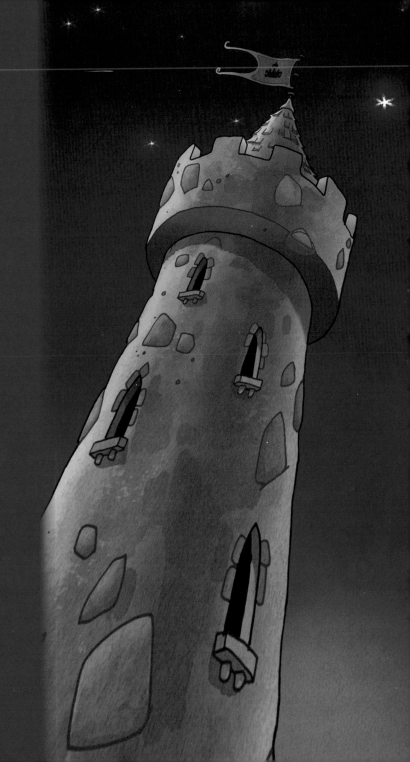

… they found a big, comfy bed!
The two knights climbed in and
went to sleep.
The End!"

Toopy's happy. He thinks he's
finished the story. But Binoo and
Mr. Dragon have other ideas.
"All right," says Toopy, "I'll
continue. The knights followed
the dragon in the forest for a long,
long time when, all of a sudden,
they saw a tower. A tower much
too tall to climb."

Before Toopy can finish his sentence, the dragon has already climbed the tower. Toopy doesn't want to follow him, but Binoo appears in a window. Toopy sighs.

"Oh fine, I'm coming."

Toopy drags himself up the far, far too many stairs.
"Ohhh, it's really high! And it's really far!"

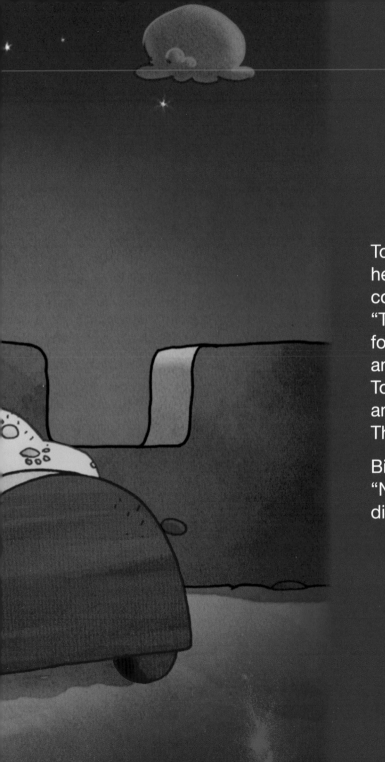

Toopy is exhausted when he reaches the top. Still, he continues the story,
"That's when the two knights found a fabulous, incredible, amazing, big, comfy bed! Sir Toopy climbed in right away and fell asleep.
The End!"

Binoo shakes his head, "No."
"No?" Toopy groans, quite discouraged.

Toopy yawns an enormous yawn, and tries again.
"How about, the two knights found a dancing octopus?
A giant duck?... Not a giant duck."

Toopy has no more ideas for finishing the story. But
Binoo does, and he whispers something into Toopy's ear.
Toopy thinks it's the best idea of all.

"At the top of the tower, the two knights found a really, really…
beautiful lady dragon. It was love at first sight for Mr. Dragon.
And for the lady dragon, too."

The dragon is happy. Binoo is happy. Toopy is happy.
He's almost finished the story.

"And, as a reward for finding the end of
the story," Toopy adds, "The two brave knights
got the most extraordinary, comfy bed!
And the two dragons lived happily ever after.
The End."

Click!

"Nighty-night Binoo."